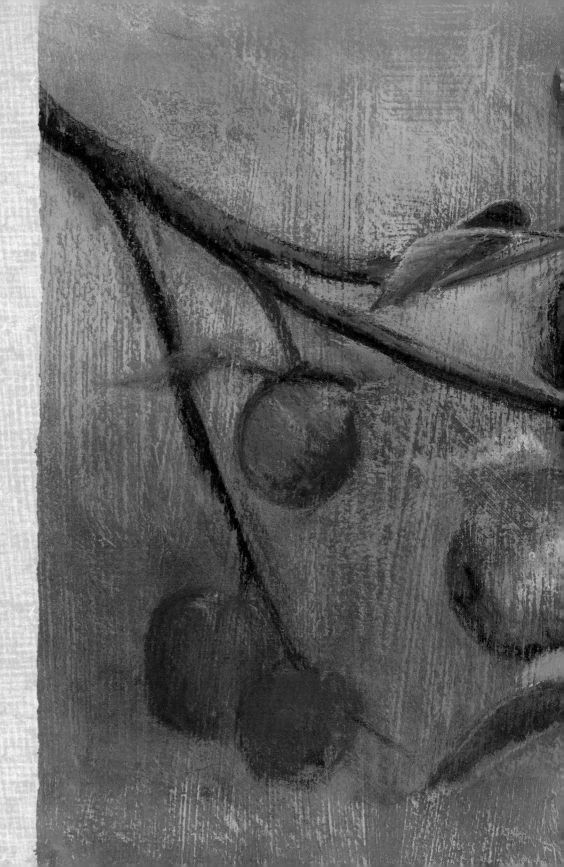

For ABC and all his grandchildren
  T.C.

For Roslyn and Phillip
  S.W.

First published 2000 by Walker Books Ltd
87 Vauxhall Walk, London SE11 5HJ

10 9 8 7 6 5 4 3 2 1

This book has been typeset in Leawood Book.

Printed in Hong Kong

British Library Cataloguing in Publication Data
A catalogue record for this book is available
from the British Library.

ISBN 0-7445-2576-4

THE GRANDAD TREE

TRISH COOKE

illustrated by

SHARON WILSON

WALKER BOOKS
AND SUBSIDIARIES
LONDON • BOSTON • SYDNEY

There is a tree
at the bottom of Leigh's garden.
An apple tree.
Vin, Leigh's big brother, said
it started as a seed
and then grew
and grew.
And Vin said
that tree,
where they used to play
with Grandad,
that apple tree
will be there ...
for ever.

Their grandad
was a baby once
and he grew
and grew.
Vin said
Grandad went to school
and he climbed
coconut trees,
and looked out at the sea
from the top.

And when he was a man
he was a husband for their gran
and a dad
for their mam
   and Auntie Melissa
      and Uncle Victor
and then
a grandad for them.

"That's life,"
   their grandad used to say.

In the spring
the apple tree
is covered in white blossom.

In the summer
the apples grow.

In the autumn
the leaves fall off.

In the winter
it is covered in snow.

And sometimes things die,
like trees,
like people ...
     like Grandad.

But they don't go away
for ever.
They stay ...
because
we remember.

Leigh planted a seed
for Grandad,
just beside the apple tree.
And when she is sad
Vin takes her hand,
and he waters the seed
with Leigh.

And it will grow and grow,
and it will go
through changes

and they'll love it
   for ever and ever ...

just like they'll always

love Grandad.